LOU KNOWS WHAT TO DO
Birthday Party

Written by
Kimberly Tice and
Venita Litvack

Illustrated by **Andre Kerry**

Lou Knows What to Do: Birthday Party
Text and Illustrations Copyright © 2017 by Father Flanagan's Boys' Home
ISBN 978-1-944882-16-7

Published by the Boys Town Press
14100 Crawford St.
Boys Town, NE 68010

For a Boys Town Press catalog, call 1-800-282-6657
or visit our website: BoysTownPress.org

Publisher's Cataloging-in-Publication Data

Names: Tice, Kimberly, author. | Litvack, Venita, author. | Kerry, Andre, illustrator.

Title: Lou knows what to do: birthday party / written by Kimberly Tice and Venita Litvack ; illustrated by Andre Kerry.

Description: Boys Town, NE : Boys Town Press, [2017] | Series: Lou knows what to do. | Audience: Children, pre-K to 5. | Summary: Lou carries a magic bubble blower that shows him what to expect at his friend's birthday party. This story is written for children in grades pre-k to 5, especially those living on the autism spectrum.--Publisher.

Identifiers: ISBN: 978-1-944882-16-7

Subjects: LCSH: Birthday parties--Juvenile fiction. | Parties--Juvenile fiction. | Social skills in children-- Juvenile fiction. | Social learning--Juvenile fiction. | Children with autism spectrum disorders--Juvenile fiction. | Autism spectrum disorders--Patients--Juvenile fiction. | Autism spectrum disorders--Patients--Life skills guides. | Children--Life skills guides--Juvenile fiction. | CYAC: Birthday parties--Fiction. | Parties--Fiction. | Social skills--Fiction. | Behavior--Fiction. | Conduct of life--Fiction. | Autism--Fiction. | Asperger's syndrome--Fiction. | BISAC: JUVENILE FICTION / Social Themes / Special Needs. | JUVENILE FICTION / Social Themes / New Experience. | JUVENILE FICTION / Social Themes / Self-Esteem & Self-Reliance. | JUVENILE NONFICTION / Social Topics / Special Needs. | EDUCATION / Counseling / General.

Classification:

LCC: PZ7.1.T546 L683 2017 | DDC: [E]--dc23

Printed in the United States
10 9 8 7 6 5 4 3 2 1

Boys Town Press is the publishing division of Boys Town, a national organization serving children and families.

To all my supportive friends and family, who have patiently listened to me talk about this project for two years and encouraged me always. Especially Lano, Mom, Dad, Aunt Kathy, and Lisa.

– Kimberly

To my parents for helping me grow into the person I am today, and to Adam for sharing this journey with me today until the end of time.

– Venita

Lou always knows what to do!

He has a magic bubble wand that shows him the future.

When he blows a bubble,
he can see what will happen.
Then he knows how to act.

Lou is going to a birthday party.
He wants to know what will happen.

Time to blow a BUBBLE!

5

Lou knows that birthday parties can be in many different places. They can be outdoors or indoors. Parties can be anywhere the birthday girl or boy enjoys spending time! Some parties are in houses, while others are at restaurants, parks, or even pools.

Lou knows that he needs to think about where the party will be when he plans how to dress. For example, Lou would look silly wearing a bathing suit to a birthday party at a restaurant.

Lou knows that he has to find the birthday girl or boy when he first gets to the party and say, "Happy Birthday!" This will help make the birthday girl or boy feel special.

Lou knows that parties can be noisy.
He may hear many different loud sounds,
such as music, talking, laughing, and more.

Lou also knows he can always ask for
a break if the noise hurts his ears.

Lou knows that many parties have themes. This means that he will see lots of decorations with the same characters or colors.

Lou knows that many parties have games. If Lou wants to join a game, he can say, "Can I play?"

Lou knows that parties are for having fun!
He should remember to smile because
parties are for being cheerful. When
people are happy, it is more fun!

Lou knows that cake is served at birthday parties. First, everyone sings the birthday song to the special person and the birthday girl or boy blows out the candles. Then it is time for everyone to share the cake.

Lou knows that when he leaves the party he needs to say goodbye to the birthday girl or boy and tell his or her parents, "Thanks for inviting me." It is also polite to say goodbye to other friends at the party.

As a guest at a birthday party, Lou showed us he knows what to do! He planned what to wear, said, "Happy Birthday," remembered to smile, and asked, "Can I play?" to join a game. Lou also knew to say, "Please and thank you."

Do you know what to do?

TIPS for Teachers and Parents on How to Use This Book

Each *Lou Knows What to Do* title is a social story that describes a situation, place, or setting that children or teenagers may find challenging. The story about Lou attending a birthday party doesn't assume the reader has done anything wrong or needs to be told what to do. Instead, the story describes what Lou does to be successful as a birthday party guest, all courtesy of his magic bubble wand.

Here are some suggested activities to help the reader apply Lou's experience to his or her own experience, with the most important contributions being your engagement and enthusiasm for the topic. Have fun!

- Prepare children for new situations (such as a birthday party) by reading this book beforehand. If the child can read independently, allow him or her to do so, and use the guide at the end of this book to check comprehension.

- If the child is not currently reading independently, you can encourage him or her to read along by saying the repeated phrase (Lou knows...) at the beginning of each page.

- Use the comprehension questions on the following pages for understanding and recall. You can alternate between presenting the questions before, during, and after repeated readings.

- Re-read *Lou Knows What to Do* as often as your child would like. Doing so will reinforce his or her understanding of the social expectations for this situation.

- You can relate the topic to your own personal experience or ask the child to tell about a time he or she had a similar experience.

- For younger children, or those with language challenges, ask them to point to images in the book or in the actual situation to increase their vocabulary and comprehension.

- Most importantly, have fun! You can even try practicing the techniques in this book so your child can feel more comfortable trying them out on his or her own.

Have fun! Consider role-playing the situations described in the story so children can become comfortable applying the strategies in their daily lives.

Show what you know!

1. **Where can a birthday party be held?**
   A. A house.
   B. A restaurant.
   C. A park.
   D. All of the above.

2. **TRUE or FALSE:** You should think about where a party is being held to know how to dress.

3. **What is the first thing you should do when you get to a birthday party?**
   A. Find the birthday girl or boy.
   B. Eat the cake.
   C. Open the presents.

4. **TRUE or FALSE:** Birthday parties can be noisy.

5. **What kinds of sounds might you hear at a birthday party?**

6. **What does "theme" mean in this book?**
   A. What someone is talking about.
   B. An idea that uses the same characters and/or colors.
   C. A music category.

7. **TRUE or FALSE:** If some people are playing a game, you can join in without asking.

8. **How should people feel at a birthday party?**
   A. Sad.
   B. Angry.
   C. Happy.

9. **What tells you someone is happy?**
   A. They are smiling.
   B. They are crying.
   C. They are frowning.

10. Explain how the cake is served, using first, next, and last.

11. **TRUE or FALSE:** You do not have to say goodbye to the birthday girl or boy when you leave the party.

For more parenting information, visit boystown.org/parenting.

BOYS TOWN
Parenting

ANSWERS: *1. D; 2. TRUE; 3. A; 4. TRUE; 5. ANSWERS VARY; 6. B; 7. FALSE; 8. C; 9. A; 10. ANSWERS VARY; 11. FALSE*

BUBBLE BONUS

Name 3 things you do at a birthday party.

Boys Town Press Books
by Kimberly Tice and Venita Litvack
Kid-friendly books that teach important life skills

A book series designed to help kids master challenging social situations comfortably and competently.

978-1-944882-14-3

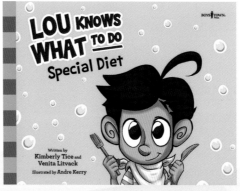

978-1-944882-15-0

978-1-944882-16-7

Each title in the *Lou Knows What to Do* series helps prepare children and adolescents to successfully navigate a unique social situation. Whether it's going to the grocery store, a friend's birthday party, or sticking to a special diet, Lou always knows what to do. Future titles in the *Lou Knows What to Do* series will address other potentially challenging social situations for readers to learn from Lou's excellent example.

BOYS TOWN®
Press

BoysTownPress.org

For information on Boys Town, its Education Model®, Common Sense Parenting®, and training programs:
boystowntraining.org | boystown.org/parenting
training@BoysTown.org | 1-800-545-5771

For parenting and educational books and other resources:
BoysTownPress.org
btpress@BoysTown.org | 1-800-282-6657